Yanni

Stable Boy of Bethlehem

Parable
Publications

by

Chandler Lanier

Published by:

Parable Publications
P.O. Box 3595
Hagerstown, MD   21742-3595
www.mcdougal.org

ISBN 1-58158-011-8

Printed in the United States of America
For Worldwide Distribution

Dedication

To my wife, Sallie.

Contents

Chapter

ONE

Life in the Stable

His name was Yallid, which is like not having any name at all, because, in Hebrew, *yallid* simply means "boy." That was all he could remember hearing: "hey, boy," "come here, boy," "stupid boy," "get out of the way, boy."

Yallid had no parents; he could not remember ever having any parents. As a newborn baby, he had been found, one cold December night, cast away into the corner of the stable, like a bag of cabbage.

Old Hannah, who cleaned the rooms upstairs, for which service she was allowed to sleep in the stable and beg food from the travelers, had found him that night. The old woman, either through her mother instinct or simply from a need to have something to fill her lonely days, had taken care of him. The townsfolk gave her enough milk to keep the baby alive.

Hannah's care for Yallid was as close to love as the child had ever received, but even these few crumbs of human kindness were taken from him when he was five years old, for then the old woman died.

Since the death of Old Hannah, Yallid had known much of loneliness, much of being cursed at and kicked about. He had known nothing of gifts, kindness or love.

Yallid was now nine years old, by the calendar, that is, but he was much older in the ways of the world. He had often been mistreated, but he had learned long ago that tears did not help. No one seemed to care how he felt. After all, he was only Yallid, the stable boy.

Yallid had no friends. He was alone — except for the animals. Ah, the animals. Many people "like" animals, and many keep animals as pets and love them — a dog, a cat or perhaps a horse. Few people, however, really "know" animals like Yallid knew animals. After all, he lived with them.

Yallid fed and cared for the animals. That's what he did in life. He even slept with the animals.

When Yallid felt lonely, he talked to the animals, and they were his fellowship. When the Bethlehem nights were cold, he snuggled up close to the animals to keep warm, and they gladly accommodated him. On occasion, when someone had forgotten Yallid at suppertime and had not called him to come get the scraps from the kitchen he commonly lived on, he even ate the grain he fed to the animals.

If animals had a language, Yallid would have been fluent in it. As it was, the animals did communicate with him, and he with them. He instinctively knew their needs and felt their burdens.

Yallid felt especially sorry for the little *hamours,*

the tiny donkeys that were the main burden bearers of the time. He knew just how they must feel.

You see, life in Bethlehem in those days revolved around three animals. Sheep were raised for their wool and their meat; goats were raised for milk, and their hides were used for tents; and the donkey was the main source of transportation. Horses were the "limousines" of the rich. Yallid was the friend of them all.

Yallid knew when the patient little donkeys had been overloaded or mistreated, and he had soothing words to calm them. He knew the places to rub so as to bring some measure of relief to their suffering.

Yallid knew the timidity of the sheep, of their fear of almost everything. He had learned the songs of passing shepherds and would sing them to the trembling animals on stormy nights.

He knew the playful antics of the goats, the clowns of the animal world. What few smiles came to Yallid were a result of watching these four-legged appetites as they scampered about. He rejoiced to care for them.

What the animals had to teach, Yallid learned,

and he learned well. Though he was uneducated in a worldly sense, his quick mind served him well. While it was true that he did not have "book learning," he was "full grown" in the lessons that life had to teach.

The stable that Yallid had to clean each day was the only one in Bethlehem. It was called a *han* in Hebrew, his language, and it had accommodations not only for travelers, but could take care of their animals too.

The inn was built in the form of a square, its open courtyard enclosed by a wall in which there was one main gate. Around the sides of the courtyard were stalls, and these contained hay and grain for the animals. In the center of the courtyard was a well from which Yallid drew water for the animals.

On the second floor of the inn were small rooms in which the travelers spent the night and a larger room which served as a dining room for all the guests.

A shepherd, for instance, taking his sheep to the Temple in Jerusalem, eight miles away, could find shelter in this inn — for himself and for his animals. The owner of the inn would meet the traveler at the gate. The guest's donkey or horse or sheep or goats would be handed over to Yallid to be fed and watered and then staked out in the courtyard. Then the innkeeper, with much pomp and ceremony, would escort the guest upstairs to his room or to the dining hall to eat before retiring.

If the night happened to be very cold or rainy, the animals would be placed in one of the stalls. Yallid himself had always slept in a stall; it was the only home he had ever known.

Suddenly, one day the inn became unusually busy. It was the thirty-third year of the reign of Caesar Augustus, master of Rome (and just about everything else), and he had commissioned a census to be taken of the entire Roman Empire. The order went out for everyone to return to the place of his birth to be counted. Yallid knew nothing about this, but he did know that now he had to run from morning to night to keep up with the feeding of the animals of the travelers. Long before nightfall every day, the inn was filled to overflowing.

One evening proved to be particularly trying. It was a cold and rainy night, and each guest demanded that his animals not be staked out in the open courtyard but be placed in stalls. There were so many animals to be accommodated that even the stall in which Yallid normally slept was needed for the stallion of a pompous rich man. The stallion proved to be every bit as haughty as his master.

Poor Yallid! Deprived of his stall, he now wondered where *he* would be able to sleep. ☆

Chapter

TWO

Visitors in the Night

When the sun went down that evening, it began to get colder and colder. Yallid tried to stay warm by huddling close to the sheep. One consolation for him was that he would surely not be called anymore the rest of the night. Because the inn was full, the owner had given orders that the gate be closed for the night. No one else was to be let in, for there was no place to put them.

Late that night, however, Yallid heard some-one knocking at the gate. He tried to ignore the sound. He was so cold and wet. Surely whoever it was would go away. The knocking continued, however, until even the manager was obliged to leave his warm bed on the upper floor. Snatching a lantern, which wasn't burning much hotter than his angry face, he shouted down to Yallid, "Well, stupid, open the gate and tell whoever it is to go away. There is no room in the inn."

Yallid made his way to the gate, slid aside the great bar that kept the gate closed against in-truders, pushed the gate open a little and peered out into the night. Before him stood a man, and beside the man he could see a woman sitting on a donkey.

"There is no room," shouted Yallid through the rain. "The inn is full. The master says, 'Go away.' "

"We must have shelter of some kind," the man pleaded, "my wife is going to have a baby, and she is exhausted. We have been traveling all day, and I'm afraid she may die if we don't find shelter."

Yallid leaned out and peered a little more

closely at the woman. Woman? She was more of a maiden than a woman. She looked to be no more than fifteen or sixteen, while her husband seemed to be in his thirties. This was in keeping with the custom of the time.

Yallid could see that the maiden was indeed very weary, perhaps to the point of fainting. She was also obviously "going to have a baby," just as her husband had said.

But what could he do? The inn was already overflowing with guests. No more room could be found upstairs. He would try to explain to them one more time.

He began again, "There really isn't any room …" But then he stopped. The maiden had lifted her face and looked deeply into his eyes.

Yallid caught his breath! He could not tear his gaze away from her face. He had never seen a face so pure, so beautiful, so loving and serene. Words failed him to describe it, and the experience shook him to his very core.

Immediately Yallid knew that he had to do something to help this man and this woman. What he could do he was not sure, but he must do something. With God's help, he would make these travelers welcome this night.

"With God's help ... With God's help ... "
Where had that thought come from? Yallid knew
nothing of religion, but he knew he must do
something now, and he needed the help of
someone greater than himself.

Yallid rushed to the stall occupied by the
great stallion. The horse, perhaps guessing
Yallid's purpose, gave a warning neigh and
even aimed a kick in the boy's direction. Yallid
quickly reached up and gripped the great horse
by the ear. Pulling the horse's head close to his
mouth, Yallid gave a shrill blast (inaudible to
the human ear) into the ear of the horse. The
horse all but collapsed. Rather than endure another such blast, he quickly bounced across the
courtyard and stood as far as possible from his
tormentor.

Yallid quickly examined the now-empty stall.
It was a little dirty, and he quickly cleaned it.

Yallid then ran to a woodpile in the corner of
the courtyard. As he ran, he grabbed the ear of a
goat and pulled it after him. He loaded wood
onto the back of the goat and thus carried the
wood back to the stall. In moments, he had a
warm fire going in the stall.

A small burro that had been carefully staked

down for the night in the courtyard somehow worked its way loose and came over to Yallid. Strangely, there were saddlebags still attached to the burro. *Why had the owner gone upstairs without them?* Yallid wondered. Looking in the saddle bags, he found bread and sausage. God had provided a meal.

"This lady must have privacy," thought Yallid, and he began to tug at a bale of hay. The hay was too heavy for him, so slowly he approached the stallion again. At first the stallion shied away from the boy. Only after calming the horse with gentle words was Yallid able to place his hand on its neck. More gentle words and more smooth rubbing of the horse's neck caused the animal to relax. Soon the stallion was nudging Yallid's hand for attention.

Yallid then was able to throw a rope over the horse's head, and together they began to drag bales of hay to the stall, where Yallid stacked them across the opening of the stall. A cozy enclosure was soon ready for the man and his wife.

Water soon filled the kettle ...What kettle? Where had it come from? One of the nosy goats had scratched it up from somewhere — just another of God's provisions that night.

Soon there was water boiling on the fire, the man and his wife were beginning to relax from their long journey, and Yallid was at peace.

Yallid had not been allowed to leave the couple, named Mary and Joseph he learned. They insisted that he stay and share the warmth of the stall and the food he had prepared. In their presence, he felt something he had never felt before. He had never known such happiness. Love seemed to penetrate every corner of the stall, and Yallid's heart was so full that he wondered if it might burst.

What was this he was feeling? He could not begin to describe it. It was glorious — whatever it was.

In that moment Yallid knew that he would do anything to help these people. When they left here, he would go with them — if they let him. He would go wherever they went, and he would serve them — gladly.

Yallid was no longer cold, no longer wet, no longer tired, no longer lonely, no longer sad. For the first time in his life he was feeling real love, and he was determined that he would never let it go — no matter what the cost.

As he thought on these things, Yallid found

himself gazing on the couple. The woman suddenly looked up and smiled at him, and Yallid was all but blinded by the radiance of her face. She was speaking to him.

"Thank you," she was saying. No one had ever said "thank you" to Yallid before.

Now the man had his arm around the boy, and he was saying, "You cannot begin to imagine how important what you have done is. May God bless you for it."

"He already has," Yallid found himself saying.

In that moment, Yallid felt overcome with joy. He was so overcome, in fact, that he decided to step out of the stall for a minute into the night air to catch his breath. Perhaps the briskness of the air and the rain on his face would cool his soaring heart.

But Yallid's heart refused to be cooled. He began twirling around and around like a top. The animals all gathered around him and were caught up in his rejoicing. Around and around Yallid spun until he fell down in a joyful heap, and there on that spot he fell into a deep sleep.

The mighty stallion moved closer and stood over the boy, sheltering him from the rain. As many sheep as could find room, snuggled up to the sleeping boy to keep him warm. As he slept, there was a grin on Yallid's face.

About midnight, Yallid was suddenly awakened from his slumber. Wasn't that the cry of a baby that he had heard? ☆

Chapter

THREE

The Baby Is Born

Yallid was now wide awake, and he heard it again. Not only was it the cry of a baby. It was the cry of a very young baby.

"The man and his wife whom I let in last night," he thought to himself ... "Could it be ... ?" And he quickly moved toward the stall where they were housed.

Before he could reach the stall, however, Yallid was stopped in his tracks. He suddenly realized how different the night was, and he looked up in amazement.

It had stopped raining, and the sky was clear. No, it was more than just clear. The sky was like crystal. Never had the moon beamed so brightly. Never had the stars twinkled so. And there were so many of them. The sky was filled with them.

"But how can the moon beam so brightly," wondered Yallid, "and the stars shine at the same time?" It was impossible, but there they were.

And where was the music coming from? There was music everywhere. It seemed that the whole world was filled with music. It was everywhere. It seemed that everything — the trees, the sky, the animals, everything – had somehow joined in joyful praise.

And what strange music! What wonderful music! Yallid heard trumpets, but they were not blasting. There were flutes, but they were not shrill. There were harps, there were cymbals, there were ... Well, there seemed to be any and every instrument he could think of, every one that he knew existed, and they were all involved in that wonderful music.

Yallid did not know much about music, but he somehow sensed that he was hearing something the world had never heard before.

And there was singing — not singing like he had ever known before. But, yes, it was definitely singing. It was just that this singing was so different. It was ... How could he describe it? It was ... glorious.

Perhaps Yallid should have been amazed by all this — dumbfounded, awestruck — but for some strange reason he wasn't. Everything about this night seemed to have been cut from some perfect pattern. It all fit together somehow. There was a rightness to it, there was a magic to it, yet at the same time, it was totally natural.

Whatever was happening was glorious. It was all joy.

"That's it," thought Yallid, "the whole world is rejoicing."

Only then did Yallid notice what the animals were doing. He had been so caught up with what was happening that he had forgotten the animals.

The sheep, the goats, the little donkeys and the great stallion were all grouped together facing the stall. They would normally have been standing here and there, doing this and that, but they seemed to be formally posed. The smaller animals were arranged in front, and the larger animals stood behind them.

He knew that these animals could often be noisy, but now they were neither quiet nor noisy. There were no distressing brays from the donkeys, no *baa*'s from the sheep, and the goats were not leaping and bumping about as they often did. Instead, they were all making soft, murmuring sounds Yallid had never heard before.

He thought he knew every sound these animals made, but what he was hearing was unmistakably new and strange. There was nothing wrong with the sounds, mind you. They were, in fact, beautiful sounds and, oh, so "right" for this wonderful night.

"Why," exclaimed Yallid, as he realized what the animals were doing. "They're worshiping! That's what they're doing!"

And so they were. From all the animals came a joyful worship, a happy praise to God, a spontaneous, perfectly normal, unaffected, expression of pure joy. And Yallid joined them and worshiped too.

Not that Yallid knew much about formal worship. He had never been permitted to go to the Temple in Jerusalem, although it was so close. Why should he go there? How could he go there? He was just Yallid, the stable boy, just a boy to be worked as long and as hard as possible, just a boy to be shouted at and scuffed about.

But, although Yallid had never before worshiped with other people, he now worshiped with the animals. ☆

Chapter

FOUR

The Coming of the Shepherds

Yallid somehow understood that the newborn baby was the reason for all this adoration, and now he timidly approached the makeshift enclosure he had fashioned for the child's parents. He could see a soft, warm glow coming from the stall, and he imagined it was from the fire he had built.

When his eyes at last fell upon the man and his wife and their baby, a great joy infused him.

This was his family now. He had adopted them just that quickly and easily, and nothing was more important than his family. "Imagine!" he thought, "having this beautiful woman for a mother and this gentle man for a father." And now he had a brother, too.

The concept of father and mother could not have meant much to Yallid except that he had watched other families who visited the inn. He had often yearned for the love he had witnessed when a mother had cuddled a little girl to her or when a father and son had shared a good laugh. "No parents could compare with these," he thought.

It never occurred to Yallid that they might reject him. He was no stranger to rejection, but somehow he knew that they were not the rejecting kind.

Yallid wasn't worried. What he had experienced already so filled his heart that he could barely contain it. Happiness was flooding his soul. Pure joy "bubbled" up out of him. No, nothing else mattered right now. He was theirs — whether they wanted him or not.

Yallid finally entered the stall, and what he saw there was love personified. The father was tenderly supporting his exhausted, yet radiant, wife. The mother was nursing her baby.

"How could so much light come from such a small fire?" Yallid wondered. It couldn't. So where was all this light coming from? He could discover no reason for it. Like the music, it was simply there. Both light and warmth existed without apparent explanation or cause.

And what was the lady doing now? She appeared to be tearing strips from old rags to wrap the infant. This glorious baby, this new brother, this beloved one was to be wrapped in dingy rags. "No! No!" thought Yallid. "This cannot be. It will not be!" And he rushed from the stall.

Yallid owned very little himself, and this included few items of clothing, but he did have one item of passable worth. At times, when the master required it, Yallid was called upstairs at mealtimes to help serve in the dining room. For these occasions, the master had given him a linen shirt. It had not been given out of kindness, mind you, but only so that the guests of the inn would not be offended by the sight of Yallid in his stable clothing.

This shirt was nothing that the average child would value, but to Yallid, it was princely.

The shirt was kept in a hollow place Yallid had discovered long ago in a wooden beam supporting the inn. After placing his shirt in the hollow, he covered the hole with a piece of old tin to discourage rats from entering it, and then he camouflaged his hiding place with straw to protect it from thieves.

The master had carefully admonished Yallid to properly care for the shirt and keep it safe and clean and had threatened his health if he failed in this regard. He was never to wear the shirt, except on these special occasions.

That he was now considering giving up his most prized possession or that he would have to face the wrath of his master when it was learned what he had done with the shirt did not pass through his mind. Without another thought, he rushed to find the shirt in its hiding place.

Yallid's first thought had been to hand the shirt, as quickly as possible, to the woman. He now realized that she would sense the sacrifice he was making and refuse it, so he began tearing the shirt into clean strips of cloth himself.

When he was ready to return to the stall and approach the woman with his gift, Yallid found that his heart was literally booming in his chest. What if the cloth was not clean enough to suit her? What if she didn't like the quality of the material? What if she refused it?

His steps seemed leaden, yet he forced himself forward. Mary needed what Yallid was offering, and he wanted to give it. Overcoming his fear, he forced himself forward and at last stood before the woman.

Yallid tried to speak, but no words came out. He tried again, but again nothing.

Mary looked up and smiled, and when she did, Yallid was undone. He could neither move nor speak now. He was simply dumbstruck.

In that moment, the mother held the baby up for Yallid to see. "Do you see how your kindness has blessed us?" she asked. "Because of what you did tonight, my baby had a warm, dry place in which to be born."

Yallid knew that he should say something, anything. "What a beautiful baby!" would have been nice, but he was somehow beyond words, and he stood staring at the miracle the woman held in her arms.

After a while, Yallid suddenly remembered his mission and, without trying to speak this time, he simply handed the strips of cloth to the woman. As he did so, he held his breath. She simply had to receive his gift. If she didn't, his whole world would collapse.

"Oh!" exclaimed the happy mother, "How could you have known how desperately I needed something to wrap my baby. You are so kind and good."

Yallid had never been called either "kind" or "good," and his heart fairly exploded. If it had been seemly, he would have done somersaults across the courtyard. As it was, he simply melted back from the stall with a silly grin on his face, leaving the mother to wrap her newborn in the clean linen.

Yallid was shaken out of his stupor by the sound of someone pounding on the gate. He again removed the bar and swung open the gate, just enough to see a group of shepherds, who themselves appeared to be in various stages of confusion. They were all trying to talk at once.

He knew these men, and they knew him.

"Yallid!" one of them shouted. "You won't believe what we have seen and heard this night!"

"There was music!" another of the shepherds shouted.

"We saw angels!" still another agreed. "We aren't crazy! We really did see them! The angels said for us to come here."

"I know," Yallid said, in an impossibly-calm voice. "Come in. There is something here that you should see." ☆

Chapter

===

FIVE

Banished

The dawn brought two great shocks to the owner of the inn. First he found a peasant couple and their newborn baby bedded down in one of his stalls.

"This will not do!" he thought. How could his inn survive the malicious gossip that would surely spread swiftly around the community that guests were staying in the stable? And how could he treat his guests respectably with a newborn baby crying so near the main entrance to the inn?

He had to do something. It was not that he was overly concerned for the welfare of either the parents or the child, but he surely did not want to be accused by his patrons of treating a mother and her newborn baby unkindly. Criticism was bad for business. He had to keep his patrons happy.

If this couple had been wealthy or important, he would have conducted them upstairs personally and would have demanded that one of his rooms be vacated immediately so that the couple could be properly cared for. He was always happy to accommodate worthy folks, but these peasants ... ?

The second shock was another "kettle of fish" entirely. Here was Yallid, his miserable stable boy, the object of his scorn and abuse over the past nine years of his wretched life, and he was now demanding — demanding, if you will — that these peasants be housed and fed.

"You will order me around, will you?" the master screamed at the boy, reaching for a stick of wood with which to knock some sense into the child's head. "Well ... , it will be a long time

33

before you are able to make that mistake again."
With this, the angry man started toward Yallid,
fully intending to carry out his threats.

So much happened next (and it all happened
so fast) that the unfortunate bully never was
able to sort it all out. It seems that the great stallion was peacefully munching on some hay
nearby when the enraged master began his attack on Yallid. As we have already seen, the
great horse had appointed himself Yallid's pro-
tector and was now ready to respond to anyone
or anything that threatened his friend. Merely a
cross word from anyone against Yallid would
have brought a negative reaction from the
horse, but to actually threaten Yallid with
physical harm … ! This was more than he could
countenance.

The horse was so offended by the master's
words and actions that he didn't pause long
enough to give a warning neigh. He rushed so
forcefully upon the angry man that he ran over
him ... simply ran over him.

The owner of the inn was now terrified, and
his attention turned fully to the majestic animal,
as the stallion turned and grabbed the offend-
ing man by the seat of the pants. Having done
this, he rendered such a bite to the man's rear

end that several weeks would go by before he was able to comfortably sit on it again.

The stallion was inclined to continue his attack, but Yallid knew that a well-placed kick from the animal could be fatal, so he intervened.

When the master saw that he was spared, he suddenly knew how he could turn the entire affair into a victory for himself. He was so enraged that he decided to rid himself at once of both his unwanted guests and his miserable stable boy. "Out! Out! Get out!" he screamed at all of them. "Go away! And never come back!"

For Yallid, no punishment had ever been so eagerly accepted. To be banished from this den of misery was to be set free from Hell. In former times, it might have alarmed him, for he would have had nowhere to go. But now, he was being banished with his newly-adopted family. He would go wherever they went. He had already made up his mind to accompany them anyway. Not only had he been released from Hell; he had been sent to Heaven, for being with them was surely Heaven on Earth.

Without fear, he accompanied his adopted parents from the stable. ☆

Chapter

===

SIX

A Home in Bethlehem

The little hamlet of Bethlehem was all astir with the news the local shepherds had spread – of the angels' song and of the birth of a miracle child. The residents of the place, being simple and rather poor folk themselves, immediately identified with the peasant couple that was expelled from the stable and threw their hearts and their doors open to them.

Yallid, because he knew the town, was able to find a vacant house they could use, and it cost them almost nothing.

Well, yes, the house was rather run down. And, yes, it did need a lot of repair to make it liveable. But then, wasn't Joseph a carpenter? It was only a matter of a day or so before the family was able to move in, and in this way, Joseph and Mary and their child took up residency in Bethlehem, and Yallid with them.

The little house was bursting with happiness. It seemed that darkness simply could not dwell there. There was light and warmth in every corner so that the house seemed to take on a life and joy of its own. As the people of Bethlehem saw this joy, they gladly adopted their new neighbors.

On the eighth day after the birth of the child, there was a frantic search in the area for a rabbi, and, as was the custom according to the ancient Law of Moses, the child was presented to him to be blessed. Yallid acted as "godfather" and proudly held the baby as the rite was performed.

As Mary and Joseph obeyed this ancient covenant with God, their child became identified as a Jew, and during the ceremony, he barely whimpered.

When the rabbi asked what name the baby was to called by, it was Mary who replied, "His name is Jesus."

"Why haven't you named him 'Joseph' after his father?" asked the rabbi.

"His name is Jesus," Mary replied again, and so he was named.

Jesus ... ! Yallid found something magical in the name, and now he loved the child even more.   ☆

Chapter

==

SEVEN

The Trip to Jerusalem

On the thirtieth day after Jesus' birth, Joseph and Mary took Him to the Temple in Jerusalem. Yallid went along and walked with Joseph, while Mary rode their faithful donkey. It was a day of great adventure for Yallid. He had never been outside Bethlehem, and every sight along the eight-mile road was something grand to him. He made exclamations about this and that as they went along.

Joseph and Mary seemed unusually joyful that day and as they made their way along the road, they began to sing:

> *I was glad when they said unto me,*
> *Let us go unto the house of the Lord.*
> *They that trust in the Lord shall be as Mount Zion*
> *Which cannot be removed, but abide forever.*

As they sang these and other promises of God concerning the Holy City, they descended steep hillsides, carefully terraced in order to utilize every possible inch of the precious soil. Golden grain waved in tiny fields. This grain was harvested to make bread, and this bread was the source of the name of Bethlehem itself.

In Hebrew, the name Bethlehem is formed from two words: *beth*, meaning "house," and *lehem*, meaning "bread." Bethlehem, therefore, literally means "House of Bread."

Later in life, Jesus would say to His followers, "I am the bread of life." It was Bethlehem, the "House of Bread," that gave Him to the world.

Sheep grazed on the hillsides of Bethlehem.

"Why," thought Joseph, "these sheep bring an even deeper meaning to the name Bethlehem." He was thinking of the name of the village in Arabic, for in that language, Bethlehem means not "House of Bread" but "House of Flesh."

It had been there, in Bethlehem, "House of Flesh," that God had become flesh to dwell among men and bring them salvation.

How carefully the Holy Spirit had selected the place for Jesus to be born! Of all the places on the Earth, He had chosen Bethlehem — "House of Bread" and "House of Flesh"!

The "road" along which the little family moved that day was more of a path than a road, and along the way they passed tiny villages of no more than three or four houses. The houses were built of stone, because stone could be found everywhere. In fact, it made the walk difficult, for man and beast alike.

"Life is difficult," thought Joseph, "like walking on these rocks, yet God can cause even the difficulties of life to bring happiness."

"These same rocks are used to build houses for shelter. They are used to build folds to protect the sheep. They are even used, when piled up like little pyramids, to collect the dew. This

41

is the only water the people have for many months of each year. How wonderfully God provides even the simplest things!"

As they walked on, they passed a flat-topped hill, the "Herodian," the hill on which King Herod was building his tomb. Most of the people hated him and prayed that he would soon have use for it. Greater sights awaited them in the Holy City. ☆

Chapter

EIGHT

Marvels Inside the Temple

On the outskirts of Jerusalem they passed many caves. In some of these caves, the outcasts of the city lived: the lepers, the cripples and the insane. These poor people would come rushing out of their caves when they saw a traveler approaching and would beg, hoping to receive something from them. Yallid had never seen anything like this in his life.

Was it Yallid's imagination, or did the infant

Jesus, turning toward these poor unfortunates, actually shed a tear?

Finally, their journey was ended, and they passed through the gate of the Holy City.

They were immediately surrounded by a sea of people, for thousands of travelers had crowded into the city for the census.

The streets of the city were narrow and were filled with shops of every kind. Shop owners, hoping for a sale, called out to Joseph. "I swear on my mother's grave that I am losing at this price. It is just that you are my dearest friend, and I want you to gain from my loss. Come! Buy!"

Joseph seemed not to hear and pushed on.

Again, Yallid had never seen anything quite like the bustle of Jerusalem. The shouting, the stench, the dust, the throngs of people … It was all a little overpowering.

Yallid was worried that the baby Jesus might be harmed by those bumping into them as they tried to get by. But they were able to pass safely.

They finally reached the great arch which supported the entryway onto the temple area. Before crossing over it, Joseph stopped to buy two small doves to be offered up as a sacrifice to

God. It was traditional to give such a sacrifice on the thirtieth day after the birth of the first boy child in each family. This sacrifice was called "The Redemption of The Firstborn." This meant that Joseph and Mary were "buying their baby back" from God. In doing so, they were making a covenant with God to raise the child to fear Him and obey His Law.

Other, more expensive sacrifices were given by the rich, but these, the humblest of all sacrifices, were all that Joseph could afford. The man who sold him the doves sneered at Joseph's poverty, but Yallid was glad that the larger animals had been spared.

They entered the Court for Gentiles and then passed on to the Court for Women. Mary would have to stay there because she was not permitted to enter the Court for Men. Before they separated, however, a very strange thing happened.

An old priest was waving to them urgently to come over to where he was. When they reached him, the old man immediately stretched out his arms for the baby Jesus. His name was Simon, and when the child was placed in his arms,

Simon beamed with joy and shouts of praise came from his mouth.

"Oh, Lord, You have kept Your word!" Simon exclaimed. "You have let me live to see Your promised Messiah! Now I can depart in peace!"

Simon then turned to Joseph and Mary and exclaimed: "Your son will cause many in Israel to be raised up. He will cause others to be cast down. He will be a light unto the Gentiles, and He will bring glory to the people of Israel."

Then, with a look of sadness, Simon turned facing Mary and said: "My daughter, your son will face danger, rejection and death. His life will be glorious, but His death will put a dagger through your heart."

"Oh, no!" Mary gasped, and she reached for the child, quickly taking him back from the priest.

"Comfort her, my son," said Simon to Joseph, "for the suffering and death of this little one is this sinful world's only hope." And he left them.

The experience left all three of them wondering, but more was to come. They had walked only a little further, when suddenly they were startled by the loud shouts of an old woman. "Praise be to God Almighty!" she was saying. "God has sent this glorious baby to redeem Israel. This is He for whom we have waited so long!"

To Joseph, she said, "Bless you, Joseph, for accepting that which you could not understand." To Mary, she said, "Bless you, Mary, for being the handmaiden of the Lord." Then she turned to Yallid. There was a blessing for him, too. His heart beat wildly as she said, "Bless you, Yallid, for the love you have in your heart for this Blessed Child!"

"How did she know our names?" Yallid asked Joseph.

"She is a prophetess," Joseph replied, "and though she is blind, God has given her the gift of seeing things that others cannot see."

The activities at the Temple concluded, and finally (and none too soon to suit Yallid), the family turned for home. Many things about the trip had not been "fun" for him, and he was anxious to get back to more comfortable surroundings. It had been a long and exciting day, but they still had the long journey back home.

Night was closing in as they approached Bethlehem, but there was light with Yallid and his adopted family. They were still basking in the promises of God given to them in the Temple in Jerusalem.   ☆

Chapter

===

NINE

The Happiest Year

The year that followed was the happiest in Yallid's life. Joseph was in constant demand in the area for his carpentry, but Yallid was also in demand. He was on call day and night to tend sick animals. "Call Yallid," was the first thought of any shepherd when his sheep or goats were injured or sick. In Yallid's hands, the sick and injured animals were assured complete recovery.

"He has healing hands," all the villagers agreed, "there is no question about that."

The little house where Yallid lived with his adopted family became the center of life in the village. People came there to share their problems or just to talk. If the truth were known, they came there just to share in the happiness and joy that filled the house. There was a glory there, and God was experienced in that humble home.

Yallid's heart constantly pounded with such joy at being part of this blessed household that he even tried to avoid sleep as much as possible because he didn't want to miss something. Every simple thing that happened in this house was something to be treasured.

Yallid loved to help Mary around the house. To him, it was pure joy. He never tired of looking into her ever-smiling face, for he felt it was her joy that had taught him to smile again. But then, he had something to smile about. Memories of his life of darkness and pain were slowly being washed away by Mary's constant tenderness.

Yallid also loved to help Joseph in his little carpentry shop, for that also brought him joy.

He counted it as a privilege, and he looked forward to it — eagerly. Joseph was no less tender and loving than Mary, and no less ready to smile and laugh.

When Joseph instructed Yallid in some skill with the lathe or chisel, the teaching was mastered quickly. Joseph was at a loss for words to express his wonder at how quickly Yallid learned. "This is the boy," marveled Joseph to visitors, "whom everyone called 'stupid.' "

But the joy of working with Mary or Joseph and learning from them, as precious as it was to Yallid, was nothing compared to the greatest joy of his life — playing with the baby Jesus. He carried the baby to see the sheep. He told Him stories about the goats. He gave Him a ride on the donkey. This became Yallid's life, and he never tired of it. As the days turned into weeks and the weeks into months, if anyone had asked Yallid what Heaven was like, he would surely have responded, "Like this."

December came, and the baby was almost a year old. Yallid wondered when Joseph would decide to take his family back to Nazareth. He had questioned Mary about it once, but such a shadow had come over her face that he had not asked again.

He had overheard Joseph and Mary talking one day. "Perhaps they will understand now and accept us," Mary had said.

"They will never understand," he heard Joseph reply. "I barely understand myself. Rather than risk your life or the life of Jesus, I would rather never go back." More recently, however, it seemed to Yallid that perhaps Joseph was having second thoughts. He had mentioned Nazareth several times.

But Yallid was not worried, and for good reason. One day he had been helping Joseph in the carpentry shop, and he had said (as lightly as possible, so as not to reveal the beating of his heart), "Father …"

Very naturally Yallid had come to call Joseph "father" and call Mary "mother." This was brought about, as much as anything, by the fact that they both began calling him "son."

"Father," Yallid asked now, "If you ever go back to Nazareth, would you take me with you?"

Joseph's head jerked up so suddenly that he banged it against a timber. His first word had to be a resounding "Ouch!" But this was followed immediately by a statement, spoken with such force that it could not be doubted. "How could you possibly ask such a question?" Joseph said, "Of course you would go with us!"

Yallid leaped at Joseph's neck, causing his adopted father to raise up again against the timber, and bringing forth another "Ouch." Joseph could not help but smile (as he rubbed the bump on his head) for seeing the joy his words had brought to Yallid's eyes.

For his part, Yallid then ran out of the shop and did a cartwheel (that somehow got all tangled up), and he ended up rolling head over heels down a little hill, winding up sitting in a tiny stream. There Yallid sat, laughing and giggling and shouting and crying all at once. After all, there is just so much happiness a ten-year-old boy can take.   ☆

Chapter

TEN

The Arrival of the Wise Men

No sooner had Yallid picked himself up from the stream than he saw, approaching down the narrow street leading to the house, three richly adorned camels. Astride the camels were three even more richly adorned riders. Gold and silver and precious stones covered their robes, as well as the camels' saddles and rigging.

Yallid had never seen anything like it. He ran

to the house, but not wanting to miss anything, hid behind the corner and peeked out at the strange men with their strange beasts approaching.

About that time, Joseph, who had also heard the commotion caused by the approaching visitors, came out of the house to greet them. They had dismounted and now approached on foot.

After a simple greeting, one of the riders asked, "Was there a baby born here in the last two years?"

"Yes," Joseph proudly told them. "His name is Jesus."

"Jesus?" mused another of the riders to his companions, "isn't that Hebrew for 'the Lord will save?' "

It was the third rider who responded: "Yes, yes, salvation … the forgiveness of sins … Perhaps this is the One for whom we have been searching."

He turned back to Joseph and announced, "We are from the province of Media in Persia. We are priests of the religion of that region. It is called 'Zorasternism,' and we have given our lives to the study of sacred scriptures. We study not only our own, but the scriptures of other faiths as well. We have found certain prophecies in the Hebrew scriptures that tell of the coming of a Messiah, a Savior, who will take away the sin of the whole world."

"Yes," broke in another of the priests, "and we were given to understand that the sign of his birth would be a great star. Five years ago, a great comet appeared in the Eastern sky, and we took this as a sign that the promised birth was near. Then, a year ago, a giant star appeared. We knew that this was a sign that the baby had been born, and we began our search. We have been following that star ever since."

"Our search has not been easy," another of the priests said. "Since Jerusalem is the holy city of the Jews, we naturally went there. And since a king as great as the star foretold would almost certainly be born in a castle, we went directly to the castle there."

"Yes, but we could not find the promised Savior in the castle of King Herod," said the first priest. "In fact, though we searched all over Jerusalem, we could not find Him in your holy city at all.

"But then, one of the scholars in King Herod's court helped us. He showed us a very old prophecy from the Hebrew scriptures that indicated that the Messiah would be born, not in Jerusalem, at all, but in 'Bethlehem of Judea.' "

When the name of King Herod was mentioned, Yallid's heart went cold as ice. He didn't know why this was, but for a moment, he felt pure terror.

"And so," continued the priest, "we started out for Bethlehem, and sure enough, the star we had been following so long reappeared, and it led us here.

"Look," he said excitedly, pointing upward, "there it is. It has stopped moving and is even now standing over this very house."

As they had been talking, daylight had been quickly fading, and now as they all looked heavenward, the great star was clearly visible to them all. They stood there staring at it for a long time.

Finally the spell was broken. "Come in," invited Joseph, "come in and see this very special baby. God told us through an angel that we would have this baby and that He would be born of the Holy Spirit. And so He was. Come and see Him."

The three priests entered the little house

where they saw Mary holding the baby Jesus in her arms. Without a word, the three visitors, with one accord, fell to their knees, touched their foreheads to the ground and worshiped Him.

"What are you doing?" exclaimed Mary, awed by the majestic bearing of the priests and their expensive attire. "Why are *you* kneeling before my child?"

"We have found him," one of the priests exclaimed, "my heart leaped within me when I looked on his face."

The three visitors then began to open packages they had brought with them for just this moment, and one-by-one they laid expensive presents at Jesus' feet.

"Here is gold," stated the first. "Gold is the symbol of royalty. This child is born a true king. Gold is everlasting, the most durable of all metals; His kingdom will last for ever. Gold is the purest of all metals, and this life will be the purest life ever lived. Gold can pass through fire and yet will not be destroyed. This child will pass though fire, yet He will remain faithful to God."

"My gift is frankincense," offered the second

priest, "this is the most costly and desirable of all perfumes. It will cover the worst of odors with its sweetness. This child's life, like frankincense, will be a sweet essence before God, covering the sins of all mankind. Through the beauty and sweetness of His life, the ugliness of this world will be made beautiful."

"And my gift is myrrh," offered the third priest. "Just as myrrh is used to heal many illnesses, this child will heal the sick, cause the blind to see, and make the lame to walk. Myrrh is also used to anoint the bodies of the dead, so this child's life will conquer death and bring men into eternal life."

After the giving of the gifts, Mary invited the three visitors to share a simple meal, and during the meal they told more about their journey to find the Savior.

After they had eaten and had fellowship together, Mary said to the three priests, "Our house is small, and I hesitate to invite you to sleep in such humble circumstances, but you are certainly welcome to spend the night with us. We would be honored to have you."

"Dear lady," one of the men replied, "never have we experienced such wealth as we found in the love of this family. We accept with grateful hearts. We are the honored ones."

Soon the visitors were shown to their resting places, and the entire household settled down for the night, still marveling at what they had witnessed.   ☆

Chapter

===

ELEVEN

The Flight Into Egypt

*J*ust before dawn, one of the priests was suddenly awakened and went to shake Joseph. "Wake up, Joseph," he called out urgently. "I have had a dream from God, and He warned me that Herod is seeking to kill the child. You must flee now, immediately, there is no time to waste. Flee toward Egypt!"

"I had just awaked myself before you called!" Joseph said. "An angel of the Lord came to me in my sleep and told me the very same thing. I must rouse the others, and we must be off quickly."

He spoke softly to Mary, instructing her to prepare herself and the child to flee. Then he went to wake up Yallid.

"We must flee, Yallid," he urged. "Herod wants to kill our baby. We must go now!"

"You don't need to convince me, Father," Yallid replied. "Now I understand why I felt panic when Herod's name was mentioned yesterday. I can be ready very quickly."

When the little family had hurriedly gathered up a few things for the journey and was ready to go out the door of the little house that had served them so well, they could not help but be concerned for their guests. "What will you do?" Mary asked.

"Don't worry about us," one of the men replied. "We will return to Media by a different route so that Herod will not find us. Thank you for your hospitality, and may God go with you."

They had said their good-byes and were about to step out the door when one of the priests turned to Yallid and asked, "Why do they call you Yallid? Doesn't 'Yallid' simply mean 'boy' in Hebrew?"

"Yes," replied Yallid," that is the only name I have ever known."

"Not anymore," Joseph spoke up, "from now on your name is not Yallid. Your name will be Yonathan, 'God has given,' for God has given you to us."

"Yonathan," thought Yallid, "yes, I like that. Yonathan, friend of David, friend of Jesus, friend of God."

Then Yallid, now Yonathan (Jonathan), helped Joseph load the few things they would carry on the donkey as Mary grasped the baby, and they rushed together out of Bethlehem toward Egypt. ☆